P9-DNM-551

A TUBA CHRISTMAS

Written by Helen L. Wilbur and illustrated by Mary Reaves Uhles

It was time for Ava to make a decision.

Ava's mother played the piano.

Plinkety-plink-plink

Her father played the violin.

Zing-zing-twing

One brother played the cello.

Zung-zung-twung

Her other brother played the clarinet.

Too-too-twee

"Ava," her mother said, "it's time for you to learn an instrument. That way, you can be ready to play with us in the holiday concert."

"Why don't you start with the piano? You can play any music on the piano," her father said.

Ava did not want to play the piano.

"Ava, play the flute," her mother said. "It's small, pretty, and easy to carry."

Ava was not interested in the flute.

"Well, how about the violin? It has the most beautiful sound, and it fits right under your chin."

Ava knew what she wanted, and it was not the violin.

"I want to play the tuba," she said.

"The **TUBA?** It's loud, brassy, and heavy. There's no tuba in our concert music."

Precisely, thought Ava, but she got her tuba lessons.

Ava's teacher was Rodney. He played the only tuba in the high school marching band. The shiny instrument coiled around him like a wonderful yellow snake, and the big brass bell flashed in the sunshine.

It was way too big for Ava to carry, but Rodney told her, "We'll start you out with a tuba that is just right for you." Rodney found a tuba that fit nicely in her lap and made her only a little lopsided when she carried it.

"We'll buy you the tuba for Christmas if you like playing it," her parents said, hoping, of course, that she wouldn't.

Ava loved her tuba: the gleaming brass, the big mouthpiece, the tube that curled and curled around and ended in the flared bell.

There was only one problem: it was easy to make **noise** but very hard to make **music**.

Every afternoon Ava practiced her tuba in her room.

bbbwwWWWWAHHHHHH

oooooomMMmmp

booooooooooffffffff

PPPrrrrrrrooo

phhhhhh
ooooOommppppp

Every evening she had dinner with her family
after they rehearsed for their holiday concert.

"How is it going, dear?" her mother would ask.
Her brothers made rude noises
and laughed at her.

"The tuba is a stupid instrument," said one brother. "You will ruin our concert."

"You are too small to play the tuba, Ava. You have to be big, like Rodney," said the other.

"Boys," scolded her father, "be nice to your sister!" That only made her brothers roll their eyes and laugh even more.

Rodney gave Ava tuba lessons at school twice a week. When Ava walked through the school halls carrying her tuba, the other kids puffed out their cheeks and yelled, "Oompa, oompa!" after her.

Rodney said, "Forget about them. The tuba is a noble instrument."

While Ava was practicing at home, she heard howling outside.

AROOOO,
AAAROOOOOO!

Their neighbor Mrs. Carter banged on the door. "Stop that noise, please!" she shouted. "It's upsetting our dog."

Ava walked through the cafeteria to her tuba lessons. One day she tripped and fell. She was not hurt, but she dropped her case. The tuba tumbled to the floor.

"Look at Ava!" the kids shouted. "She tripped over her own tuba." They seemed to think this was very funny. That was it! Ava had had enough.

At her lesson with Rodney, Ava said, "I'm quitting."

"That's too bad," said Rodney. "Just when you were going to be in a concert."

"A concert?" asked Ava.

"Yes," said Rodney. "A very special holiday concert, the first one of its kind held in this area." Then he told her all about it.

"Really?" asked Ava.

"Yes," said Rodney.

"That's wonderful," said Ava.

"I know," said Rodney. "Should I give you five tickets so you can bring your family?"

"Just four, please," said Ava. "I had better get practicing."

And that's what Ava did—
she practiced.

The notes came a little easier and sounded just a bit better every night.

Her horn seemed just a little lighter as she carried it.

Posters announcing the **Surprise Holiday Concert** appeared in her school.

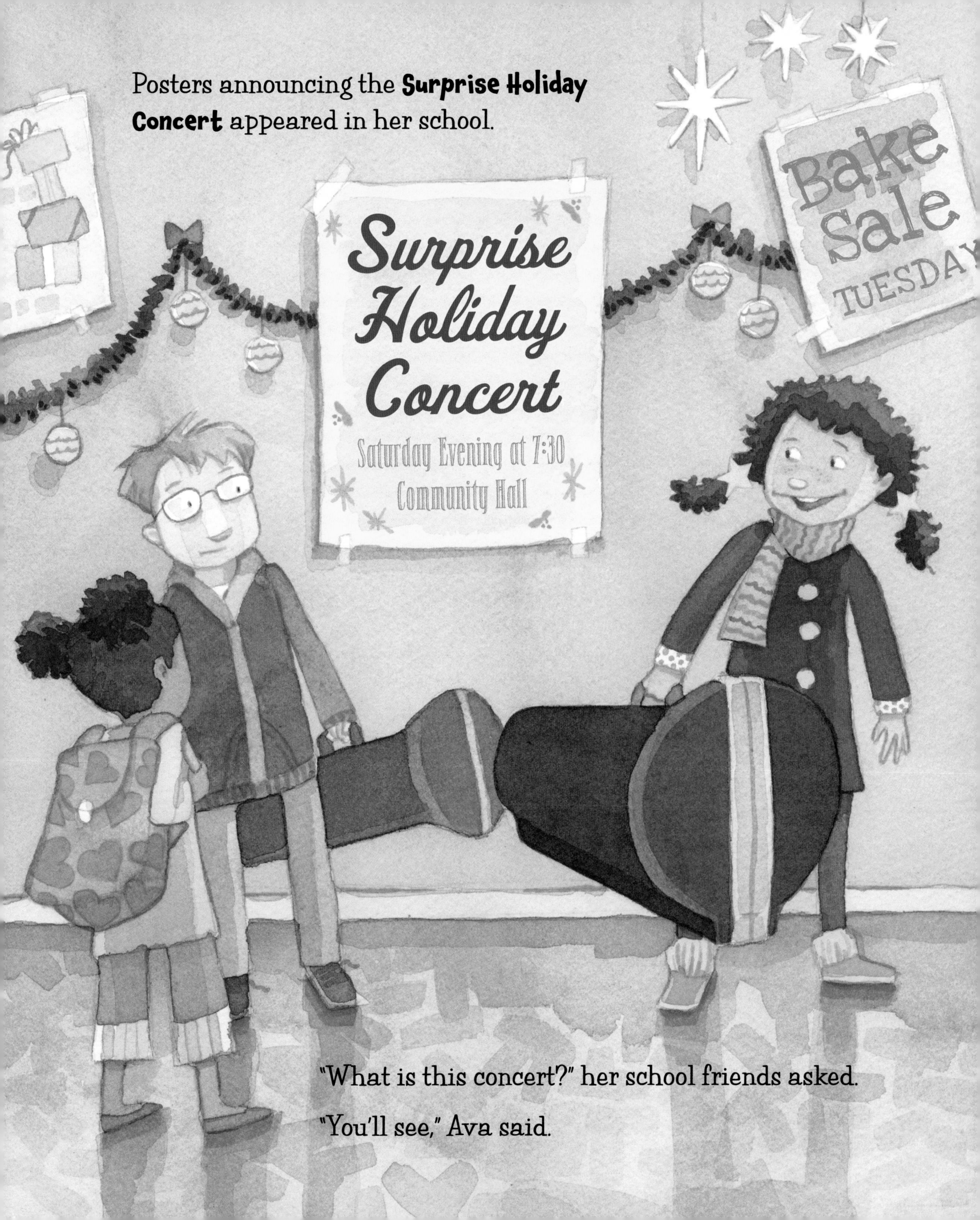

"What is this concert?" her school friends asked.

"You'll see," Ava said.

"You can't be in a concert," her brothers said. "Your playing stinks. You hit wrong notes."

The next day Ava asked Rodney, "What if I play wrong notes?"

"Don't worry," said Rodney. "We are playing in an ensemble, which means together with other players. If someone misses a note, other players will hit the right one and no one will know. It's a great chance to learn."

The day of the concert came.

Her father dropped her off for the rehearsal and said, "Good luck, Ava. You know, if this doesn't work out, you can always play the flute."

Ava entered the auditorium. The butterflies in her stomach flew away as she saw that there were tubas—tubas *everywhere*. The players were all dressed up and even the tubas were decorated.

"Come on over, Ava." Rodney had a box of decorations. He found her an elf hat and helped her trim her tuba.

The auditorium doors opened and people rushed in.
"What?" some said. "Tubas, that's it?"

Kids from Ava's school laughed,
covered their ears, and said, "Oh no!"

Ava's brothers pretended
not to know her.

Rodney stood in front and said, "Welcome, everyone, to our first Tuba Christmas." He explained that the tubas would play each song twice—once for the tubas alone, and then a second time for everyone to sing along.

Then the tubas started. The notes—low and round and rich—floated through the auditorium, and people began to smile.

"Jingle Bells." Everyone knew the words—first one person, then another. Soon, the whole audience was singing along with the music. They played and sang "Frosty the Snowman" and other holiday songs.

The concert was **loud** and it was **fun**.
At the end everyone cheered and cheered.

Ava could see her brothers pointing and saying, "That's Ava, our sister!" Kids from her school waved and took her picture.

After the concert Rodney called Ava over. "You did a great job today, Ava!"

Ava's mother, father, and two brothers stood there smiling. Her father held out a bright, shiny new tuba. It was just the right size for her.

For the new musician in our family—
Merry Tuba Christmas!

WHAT IS A **TUBA** CHRISTMAS?

Tuba players the world over put everyone in a holiday spirit with annual Tuba Christmas concerts. Tubist Harvey Phillips started the tradition in 1974 with a concert in Rockefeller Center in New York City to honor his tuba teacher, William Bell, who was born on Christmas Day in 1902. The tradition grew and spread. Every holiday season all around the world, from Disneyland to Switzerland, tuba players of all ages delight audiences with a medley of holiday favorites.

The tuba is the lowest-pitched and largest brass instrument. Tubas come in various sizes and keys. Players make a buzzing sound into the mouthpiece and use the instrument's valves to create the musical notes. If you uncoil a tuba, you'd get around sixteen feet of brass tubing. Any musician who plays an instrument in the tuba family, which also includes euphoniums (you-phone-ee-ums), sousaphones (soo-sa-phones), and baritone horns, can participate in Tuba Christmas. Find one near you. It's loud, it's fun. . . . It's just plain glorious.

For Barbara, Martha, Melanie, and,
of course, for Vivian, who gave me the idea

—Helen

For the teachers and students of the Oliver Middle School band in
Nashville, Tennessee, who helped me bring Ava and her tuba to life

—Mary

Sleeping Bear Press™
2395 South Huron Parkway, Suite 200
Ann Arbor, MI 48104
www.sleepingbearpress.com

Printed and bound in the United States.

10 9 8 7 6 5 4 3 2 1

Library of Congress Cataloging-in-Publication Data

Names: Wilbur, Helen L., 1948- author | Uhles, Mary, 1972- illustrator. Title: A tuba Christmas / written by Helen L. Wilbur ; illustrated by Mary Reaves Uhles.
Description: Ann Arbor, MI : Sleeping Bear Press, [2018] | Summary: "When Ava decides to learn to play the tuba, it isn't as easy as she thought it would be. But with the encouragement of her music teacher, Ava finds a place for her and her tuba in a special holiday celebration"— Provided by the publisher.
Identifiers: LCCN 2018006619 | ISBN 9781585363841 Subjects: | CYAC: Tuba—Fiction. | Concerts—Fiction. | Perseverance (Ethics)—Fiction.
Classification: LCC PZ7.W6413 Tu 2018 | DDC [E]—dc23
LC record available at https://lccn.loc.gov/2018006619

I like minty
toothpaste.
Strawberry is
for babies.

For Ayeishah

First U.S. edition 2016

Library of Congress Catalog Card Number pending
ISBN 978-0-7636-8943-8

16 17 18 19 20 21 FGF 10 9 8 7 6 5 4 3 2 1

Printed in Shenzhen, Guangdong, China

This book was typeset in Baskerville.
The illustrations were created digitally.

Nosy Crow
an imprint of
Candlewick Press
99 Dover Street
Somerville, Massachusetts 02144

www.nosycrow.com
www.candlewick.com

Christmas
for Greta and Gracie
Did you know that Santa Claus eats marshmallows for breakfast?
Yasmeen Ismail

Greta and Gracie were sisters.

Greta was bigger because she was one year, six months, and three days older than Gracie. They both had the same smile, the same hoppity-skip walk and their names both began with G, too. But . . .

When I was your age,
I was much taller than you are
now. I could even reach the kitchen
counter on my tippy-toes!
It's nice being taller. It makes me look
more elegant, don't you think?
Anyway, it must be hard being
SO short....

. . . Greta was chitty-chatty and Gracie was quiet.

That was just fine because

Greta loved talking to Gracie,

and Gracie loved listening.

Most of the time.

It was Christmas Eve, and Greta and Gracie were busy coloring.

Greta had the red, green, yellow, blue, AND black crayons.

Gracie had the brown crayon.

Gracie was still coloring.

She wanted her picture to be just right.

So Greta and Gracie put on their jackets and went to help decorate the big tree in the village.

Gracie found the star in the big box of decorations. She was just getting ready to climb the ladder and put it on the tree when Greta came over.

I'll do it, Gracie.

You're too LITTLE and I've climbed ladders before. I'll put it on the tree, and then we'll go to the store.

So Greta put the star on the top of the tree.

The store was very busy. Gracie wanted to buy some red ribbon for wrapping presents, but it was too noisy.

So Greta asked for the gold ribbon.

Mrs. Goose chatted to Gracie as she carefully counted out her coins.

You must be excited about Christmas, Gracie.
What do you think Santa is like?

Oh! Santa is just WONDERFUL!
He is the best and nicest man, and he has a sleigh and reindeer, and he gives presents to good little girls and boys, and he has a HAT and a red coat and a big white bushy beard, and he eats COOKIES!
You can write him a letter and he'll come and visit and say "Ho! Ho! Ho!" and he puts things in stockings and he wears black BOOTS and he has BIG buttons on his coat....

He is magic.

On the way home, Greta said they should go ice-skating.

Let's go fast!
Can you twirl as quickly as me?
No, Gracie! Like this! Like this!

And now stand on one leg!

Like this!

Like this!

And stretch your arms!

Like this!

Like this!

Like this!

But Gracie decided to go very slowly on the ice.

I don't like going fast—
it makes me feel wobbly
in my tummy. I might fall over.
Do you think Santa
likes to skate?

Santa is a champion skater. But Gracie, you're still not doing it right! Do it fast! Faster!
Oh, I'll do it by myself. You're too SLOW.

That night, Gracie was listening to Greta snore when she heard a funny noise.

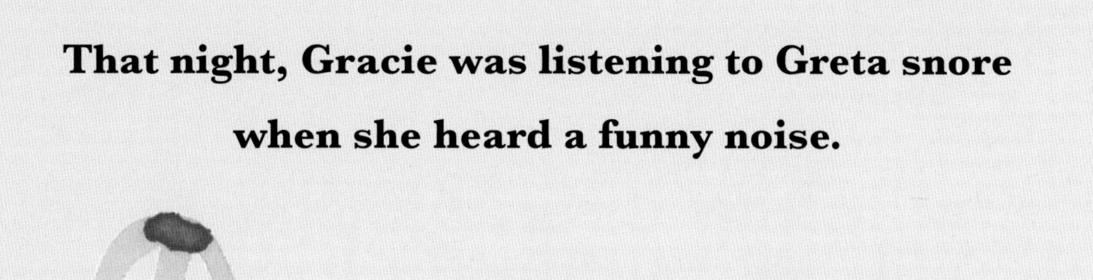

Could that be Santa?
I must not wake up Greta. It's good to be SLOW.

Gracie slipped out of bed and opened the bedroom door very carefully so it didn't squeak.

She tiptoed along the hallway
so her feet didn't make a single sound.
I must not make a noise. It's good to be QUIET.

The living-room door was open a tiny bit,
and Gracie squeezed through the crack.

I can just fit through. It's good to be LITTLE.

And there, through the doorway, she saw . . .

Hello, Gracie! What a good thing that you're here. Would you like to help me?
It's you!

Santa Claus!

So Gracie helped Santa with all the presents. Then they ate cookies, drank milk, and talked about all sorts of things until it was time for Santa to go on his way.

The next morning, Greta woke Gracie up very early.

He came!
He was here, Gracie!
The cookies have all been eaten, so he must have liked them. And there are lots of presents under the tree. I haven't counted them all, but there are a lot. I hope the big ones are for me! We've both got full stockings, too. . . .

Around the tree were two full stockings and a pile of presents.

Look! This one's for you, Gracie. I'll read the label.

Dear Gracie,
Thank you for your help.
It was very nice to meet you. Love, Santa

You met Santa Claus?

For Gracie

Yes, I did. He was sitting right here and he had BROWN boots and a red coat and a big sack full of presents that had red ribbon and gold ribbon and blue ribbon and green ribbon and ALL THE RIBBONS!
And he told me all about his reindeer and what they like to eat and he was really nice, and he had a big white beard and twinkly eyes, and he asked me to help him!
Come on, Greta, let's open our presents....
For Greta

And for once, Greta did not say one single word.

Merry Christmas!

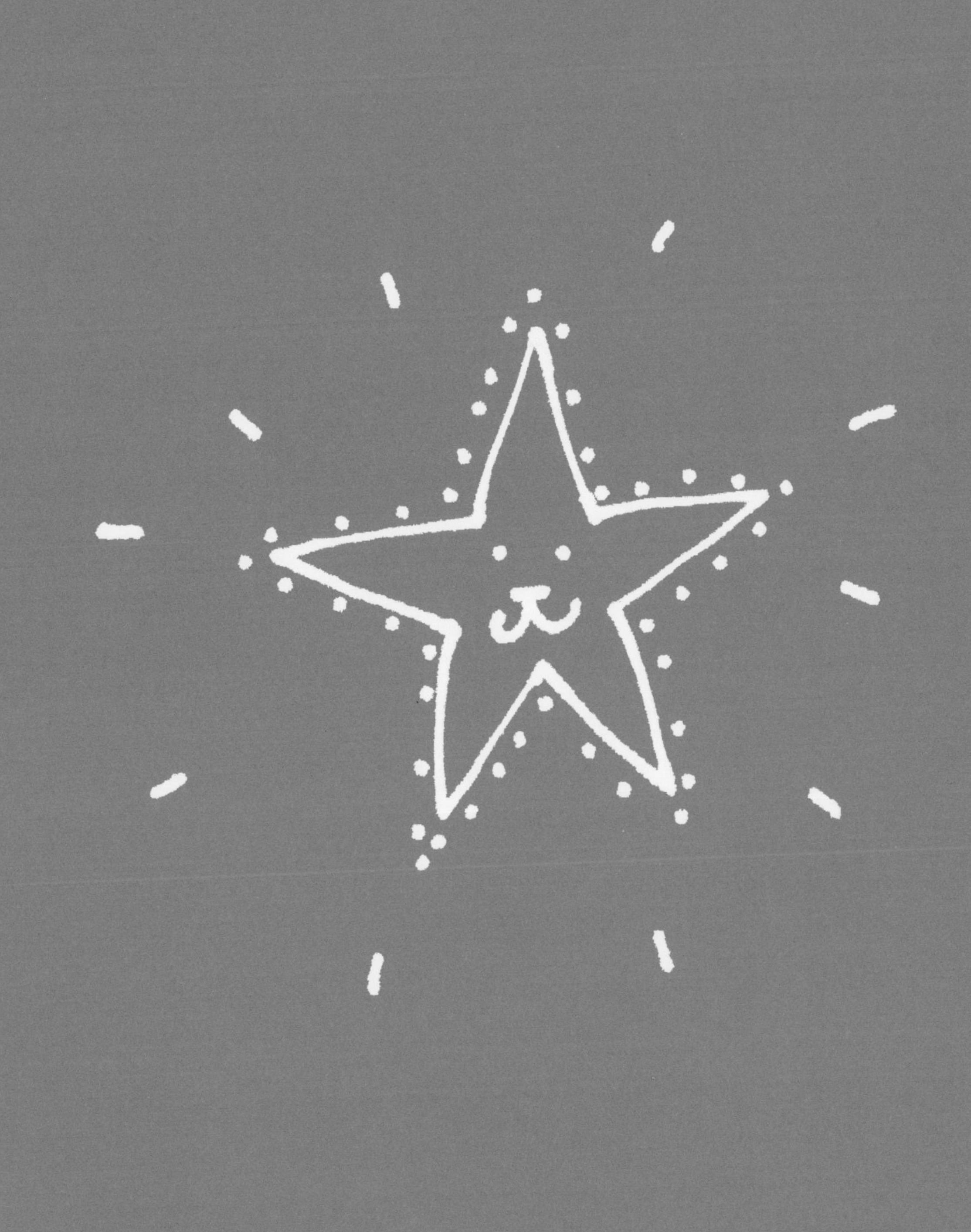